Van Dog

Story by ***Mikołaj Pa***
Art by ***Gosia Herba***

Milky Way
Picture Books

HOCKNEY
VAN RUISDAEL
Pierre Bonnard
PIETER BRUEGEL
VAN GOGH
William Turner
MONET
PAOLO UCCELLO

For Jan and Agnieszka
— G.H.

For Pola and Ella
— M.P.

Van Dog

Copy editing by Nick Frost
Translation by Mikołaj Pa
Book design by Mikolaj Pa
Additional design for this edition by Jolin Masson

This edition published in 2022 by Milky Way Picture Books,
an imprint of Comme des géants inc. Varennes, Quebec, Canada.

Library and Archives Canada Cataloguing in Publication

Title: Van Dog / Mikołaj Pa; illustrated by Gosia Herba.
Names: Pasiński, Mikołaj, author. | Herba, Gosia, illustrator.
Identifiers: Canadiana 20220010188 | ISBN 9781990252129 (hardcover)
Classification: LCC PZ7.1.P37 Va 2022 | DDC j823/.92—dc23

ISBN: 978-1-990252-12-9

Printed and bound in China

Milky Way Picture Books
38 Sainte-Anne Street
Varennes, Qc J3X 1R5
Canada

www.milkywaypicturebooks.com

OIL
TURPEN-
TINE

MUSEUM

RING!
RING!

WHAT A BEAUTIFUL DAY TO PAINT!

CLICK
TWEET
TWEET
BUZZ
BUZZ
CLICK
BUZZ
BUZZ
TICK
TICK
TICK
TICK
BEEP
BUZZ?

SCREECH
BUZZ
HUMM
TICK
TICK
HOOF

GOOD MORNING!

WHAT ARE YOU DOING?

CAN I LOOK?

CLUNK
QUACK
BAAA
BAAA
BAAA
BAAA
HISSS
WHOOSH
OOOO!
GRUNT

CAW
CAW
WOW! HOW NICE!
BUZZ
HUFF HUFF
HISSSS

TWEET
QUACK
PSHAW!
OM NOM

CHOMP!
HMM...

ZOOOM
ZING!
WHIZZZ
GOOOOOOAL!
BAAA
BA!
BAAAA
BAAA BAAA
BAAA
BAAA
BAAA?
BAAA!
GOT IT!
WEEE
CHOMP
CHOMP
GRUNT
HISSS
LAST NIGHT I DREAMED THAT I FLEW INTO SPACE.
ANTS, GATHER UP!
AAAA!
DID YOU?
OOPS!
AAAA!

BAAA
MEOW?
EXCUSE ME, WHAT TIME IS IT?
SHHH... PLEASE DON'T DISTURB.
BAAA
OH, THIS MUSHROOM LOOKS TASTY.
HOOF!
HISSSSS

ZOOOM
CHIRP
OUT OF THE WAY!
YOU'RE LATE...
I'M SO SORRY.
BAAA
BAAA
BAAA
BAAA
BA!
BAAA
BAAA
BAAA
BAA
HAHA!
MUNCH CHRUNCH
PFFFFT!
ONE!
IT WAS A-MAZ-ING! THE MEADOW SEEMS SO TINY FROM UP THERE.
COUNT OFF!
THREE!
HISSS

CACKLE
CACKLE
ARE YOU A BIRD?
NOPE.
PSSST.
ACHOO!
PSSSSSST.
CHEEP. CHEEP.
BAAA
BAAAA
CLUCK CLUCK
SLURP
YUCK!
HOOF, HOOF!
TWO!
MMM, SO YUMMY.
ZZZZZZZZZ
OM NOM

ZOOOOOM
TWEET
TWEET
CAN I COME
WITH YOU?
BAAA
BAAA
BAAA
BA
BAAA
BAAA
BAAA
BAAA
BAAA
BAAAAA
BAAA
BAAA
BAAA
BAAA
BAA
OM NOM
NOM

WHICH WAY TO TOKYO?

CAW CAW

I'M HUNGRY.

SHALL WE HUNT SOME FROGS?

MEOW.

GO STRAIGHT AND THEN TURN RIGHT!

IT'S VERY FAR...

MAKE WAY!

YOU MAKE WAY!

IT'S GOING TO RAIN.

BAAA

BAAA

BAAA

BAAA

SOB.

ZZZZ

BAAA

BAAA

ARE YOU A BIRD?

I'M A PIG.

QUICK! I'M GETTING WET.
I LIKE RAIN.
I DON'T.
HEY, WAIT FOR ME!
RIBBIT RIBBIT
WEEE!
SPLASH
IT NEVER RAINS IN SPACE.
NEVER?
YAWN
YAWN

HOO, HOO.
BOO
ZZZ...
CLIP
CLOP
EEK
EEK
ZZZZ
BOOORING...

TOO
TOO
TWEET
TWEET
BEEP
BOOP
GOOD AFTERNOON!
HOW DO YOU DO?
MY NAME IS DUMPLING.

WHAT ARE YOU PAINTING HERE?

GOSH!

WHAT A NICE BLUE!

CAN I SMELL IT?

I ADORE THE COLOR BLUE!

I KNOW MANY KINDS OF BLUE:

UL-TRA-MAR-INE, INDIGO, EGYPTIAN BLUE, CORNFLOWER,

MIDNIGHT BLUE,

TURQUISE, TEAL, NAVY, COBALT, SEA BLUE, LAPIS LAZULI, DEEP BLUE, AZURE, SAPPHIRE, CYAN.

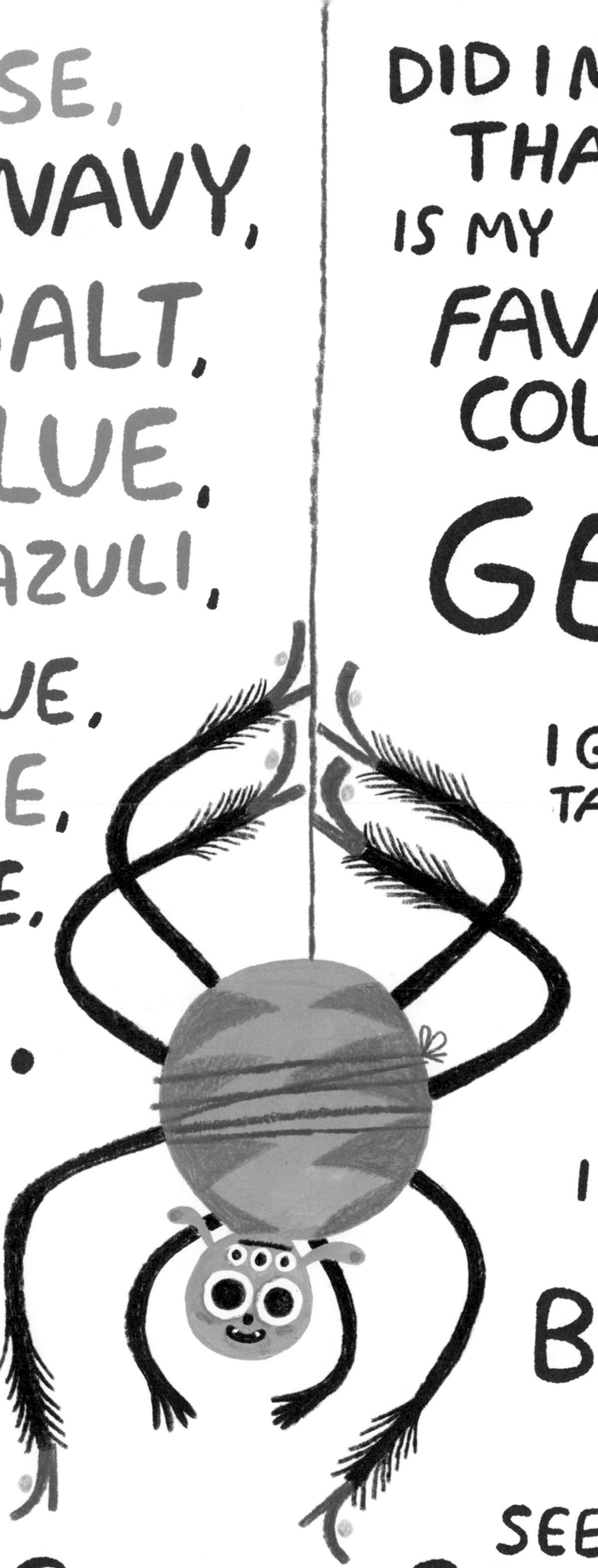

DID I MENTION THAT BLUE, IS MY FAVORITE COLOR?

GEE...

I GOT TIED UP TALKING BLUE AGAIN.

IT'S SOOOO LATE! I HAVE TO GO.

HMM, YES... WHAT WAS I SAYING?

BYE THEN! SEE YOU! SO LONG!

QUACK
CHIRP CHIRP
ROAR!
!!!
ARE YOU A BIRD?
ZZZZZ
???
TUTUUT TUTUUT
HAS IT BEEN RAINING?
HE'S NOT LOOKING, RUN!
I'M A BEAUTIFUL BUTTERFLY!
THIS IS SOME WEIRD BOOK.

DIP DIP
TICK TICK
ARE THEY BITING?
GET AWAY FROM ME!
BUZZZ
ZZZZZ
GET A LOAD OF THAT RAINBOW!
LEFT, RIGHT, LEFT, RIGHT...

BAAA
BAAA
WEEE!
OOO!
HOP!
ICE CREAM!
THUMM
THUMM
THUMM
THUMM
THUMM
THUM
BANG
RAT
TAT
CRASH
CRASH
ZING
ZIIIING
BOOM
BANG!
GONG
BOM
TICKA
TICKA

WHUP-WHUP-WHUP
WHUP-WHUP-WHUP
TA!TA!
TADAAA
OWOOOOOOO
OOOO!
LALALA
PLINK
PLINK
PLINK
RATTLE
RATTLE
RATTLE
RATTLE
SPLASH
PLOP
PLINK
PLINK
PLINK
PA
RUM
PUM
PUM

GOOD TO BE BACK ON EARTH.
BE PATIENT.
EASY, FOLKS, THERE'S ENOUGH FOR EVERYONE.
CONE?
I'M HUNGRY!
WHAT ARE YOU HAVING?
EIGHT CHOCOLATE SCOOPS.
PINK!
I SCREAM, YOU SCREAM, WE ALL SCREAM FOR ICE CREAM!
YOU PLAY SO WELL, MY DEAR GRANDSON.
SOMEBODY IS WATCHING US.
A COMET IS COMING AT US!
I WONDER IF THEY HAVE TOMATO FLAVOR...
DON'T STARE, SON. THESE ARE REAL VAMPIRES.
DA... DAD?

I LOVE ICE CREAM!
AHEM!
YUMMY
YOU ARE MY BEST FRIEND.
FIRST THE ALIENS, NOW A COMET. WHAT NEXT?
VANILLA IS THE BEST FLAVOR.
WILL YOU BUY ME SOME ICE CREAM?
YOU MEAN POTATO.

MOVE OVER, BIG GUY!
YEAH, MOVE IT.
AHOY!
UP WE GO!
HOW DID YOU CLIMB UP THERE?
WOO!
WOO!
THE FLOOR IS LAVA!
HELP!

EXCUSE ME, HAVE YOU SEEN A GIANT LIZARD PASS BY?

BOOHO,
SUCH A BEAUTIFUL
SUNSET...

GEORGE! IT'S HOME TIME!

FANCY A MARSH-MALLOW?

WEEEEE

HOWWWL!

CLICK

HA HA

SHEESH! THEY MADE A MESS AGAIN!

ZZZZ

AAA!

MRRRR

SSSSSSS

ZZZZZ

HOO
HOO
ZZZZZ
IT REMINDS ME OF PICASSO.
BUT I'D PAINT IT BETTER.
WATCH YOUR FINGER, MISTER!
YAWN
PSSS
ZZZZZZ
ZZZZZ
ZZZZZ
ZZZZ
ZZZZ
ZZZZ
ZZZ

IS IT FINISHED?

YES!

RING
RING

MUSEUM

BELLO!

HOCKNEY
VAN RUISDAEL
HA
HA
CHOMP
CHOMP
Pierre Bonnard
PIETER BRUEGEL
VAN GOGH
William TURNER
MONET
PAOLO UCCELLO

HOW PRETTY!

*
*THE END

PHIL